This innovative project encourages children ages seven to twelve to become "emotional ecologists," determined to work to become more responsible as they grow up, leave a better world for those who follow them, and help a new generation develop.

It is an open invitation to reflect, debate, develop creatively, and share experiences that allow personal improvement. Only if we are aware that something has value will we defend it, take care of it, respect it, and then watch it grow.

We hope you enjoy this innovative concept as you embark on an exciting exploration of yourself and the world around you!

To Zulma and to the whole generation of CAPA children.

HOW DOES THIS BOOK WORK?

The content is purposefully open, leaving space for mentors and teachers to enrich the activities and ideas in their own way.

The book consists of five chapters that follow the same structure:

Each chapter begins with a double page of illustrations and poses three questions. These three questions are visually reflected in the illustrations, sparking debate and an exchange of opinions on the chapter's theme. This encourages learners to "see" and "read" much more than what appears on the printed page.

Presenting a parallel or analogy between the world around us and our inner world, this double-page spread uses text and illustrations to examine what we call "emotional ecology." This approach will help us to better understand what is happening inside us, what the causes are, and any consequences that may arise.

These two pages encompass both environmental education and emotional education; one concept complements and enriches the other, allowing us to develop and better understand both of them.

Now that we have identified what happens inside us and what the consequences may be, the **third double-page spread encourages us to think** about how we can act differently and better adapt ourselves. Full-page illustrations again serve as an invitation to participate and ask questions, further engaging students and proposing possible tools and solutions that will help them realize their objectives.

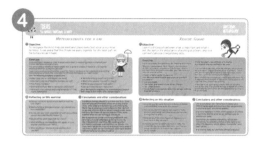

The six proposals put forward in each chapter (through activities, stories, games, or hypothetical situations) **allow us to work on the skills we need to overcome the obstacles identified therein,** helping us to become stronger and more emotionally ecological.

A brief guide for mentors accompanies each scenario, allowing them to tailor the activities to a group or situation.

Each exercise follows the same structure and consists of four distinct sections: an objective that addresses the scenario; an explanation of the scenario; reflections on the exercise; and conclusions that can be drawn for further investigation.

If you like the proposed scenarios and think that they could be useful, we invite you without further ado to become meteorologists for a day. Rein in your behavior and learn how to control yourself; make a beautiful umbrella to protect you from all kinds of "rain," working in every way possible toward becoming a sustainable and creative person.

SUMMARY

EMOTIONAL METEOROLOGY

- WHAT IS METEOROLOGY?

- WHAT'S THE WEATHER LIKE WHERE YOU LIVE?

- DID YOU KNOW THAT YOUR INNER TERRITORY HAS ITS OWN METEOROLOGY?

?

5

Climate diversity

creates different landscapes and ways of living. Living beings adapt to the environments they inhabit and develop mechanisms to survive in both extreme cold and heat (the Poles and deserts). There is much beauty in this diversity. Have you noticed how beautiful a blue sky dotted with white clouds can be? It suggests all kinds of shapes and figures. And who has not admired falling snowflakes during a heavy snowfall?

Every meteorological phenomenon arouses some emotion in us: Rain can be associated with melancholy, snow with the desire for fun (making snowmen!), a rough sea with huge waves may make us feel afraid.

✸ Let's reflect...

- Who hasn't been frightened during the thunder and lightning of a heavy storm, when it seems as if the sky is about to fall on our heads?

- A light breeze can be very pleasant, but a hurricane not so much.

- Did you know that a tropical hurricane's winds can reach speeds greater than seventy-three miles per hour?

Emotional climate is the result of the emotions we receive from all the people who share Earth's ecosystem. There are many different phenomena in emotional meteorology. Let's look at some of them more closely.

Rain in the heart: Sadness, tears, sorrow, problems – too much rain can cause a flood inside of us.

Thick emotional fog: Unpleasant and gray, it seems to come up from the ground, rising into the sky before settling down and covering the landscape. It stops us from seeing where we're going. We feel lost and alone.

Hurricane-force winds: Everything that seemed to be running smoothly and was safe and secure quickly disappears, leaving us feeling powerless and bewildered.

Clear and sunny skies: We must enjoy these moments when everything seems to be in its place. Sometimes we don't value or appreciate them enough.

Let's reflect...

- Which emotional meteorological phenomena occur most often in your inner territory?

- Are there any you are really afraid of?

- How do you respond when you feel out of control?

- And if another person is out of control, how do you react?

7

HOW CAN YOU
MAKE THIS HAPPEN?

METEOROLOGISTS FOR A DAY

☼ Objective:

To recognize the most frequent emotional phenomena that occur in our inner territory. To be aware that the climate we enjoy depends, for the most part, on the territories we inhabit.

Exercise:

Each participant receives a sheet of paper with a chart of weather symbols on the back, and is given the following instructions:

You are a famous emotional meteorologist who is going to prepare a report on your interior emotional weather during the last year.

Draw a picture of yourself based on a weather chart on the back of the worksheet, drawing the meteorological symbols that represent the different phenomena you experienced.

Use the following questions to guide you:

- How many days of sunshine did you have?
- How many rainy days? Was the rain heavy or light?
- Was there a rainbow?
- Did the wind blow? Was it a breeze or a hurricane?
- What was your average emotional temperature? Cold, warm, temperate?

- Were there foggy days? Did it snow?
- What is the weather forecast for today?
- What do you predict for next week?
- Are your forecasts ever inaccurate?

Once the task is completed, the meteorologists present their maps to the others and a debate begins.

⊛ Reflecting on this exercise

- Can you say which global environment is most like your chart?
- What emotional phenomena occur most often in your inner territories?
- Do you like your inner emotional climate? Do you think you can do something to improve it?
- Do any of the other maps look like yours?
- What emotional phenomena did not appear on your weather chart last year? Why?
- What would your ideal emotional weather chart look like?

⊛ Conclusions and other considerations

Emotional changes abound in our inner territory. Some days are gray and overcast; others are sunny and full of joy, while some are darkened by a disorienting fog. There may be downpours and hailstorms that can hurt us, or days when we find ourselves living in a cold, lonely territory. But there will also be periods of fine, warm weather when we can feel happy and secure.

We all experience similar emotional phenomena, and although we would sometimes prefer to live in only the most pleasant conditions, life situations affect our interior landscape, and therefore our climate. It is important that we are prepared and know how to protect ourselves so that we can live through all kinds of weather without losing our emotional balance.

RESCUE SQUAD

⊕ Objective:
Learn to distinguish between what is important and what is not. Recognize the importance of working as a team. Improve communication and negotiating skills.

Exercise:
Form four groups. Give each group the following information:

You are a rescue squad. Your mission is to respond to an SOS call from an area inaccessible to road vehicles. Although there are twenty evacuees, your helicopter can only carry ten at a time.

- **Seven children under 10 years old.**
- **An 80-year-old woman in good physical condition.**
- **A dentist.**
- **A psychologist.**
- **The father and mother of one of the children.**
- **The child's teacher.**
- **Two prisoners who have escaped from jail (one suffering from dehydration).**
- **Four teenagers, two of them with injuries.**
- **A migrant who has worked in the area.**

You have thirty minutes to decide who you will prioritize for evacuation. The decision must be unanimous. Those who are not rescued will have to wait more than twenty-four hours until the next rescue attempt.

Make a list of the evacuees you would give preference to, numbering them in order of one to ten, and explaining why you think they should have priority.

When time is up, each group shares their list with the rest of the class. The mentor initiates a debate about the results and any difficulties the participants had coming to their decisions.

⊕ Reflecting on this situation
- How did you feel about having to make such difficult decisions? What criteria did you consider?
- How do you think the people who wouldn't fit into the helicopter would feel? How would you feel after leaving them to wait?
- What do you think might happen if someone loses their nerve in that situation?
- How did you feel about discussing this within the group? Do you feel people listened to you? Did any group members try to impose their opinions on the others?

⊕ Conclusions and other considerations
Life is not always fair. Sometimes it places us in difficult landscapes and situations that can generate explosive or toxic emotional weather.

It is very important to know which values to prioritize in our lives, and the price we are willing to pay to achieve our goals.

Sometimes, by wanting everything, we can lose everything. No possible solution seems right to us. When this happens, we can always choose the "least bad" option.

It is vital to make our decisions without prejudice.

RAIN IN MY HEART

✲ Objective:

Understand the nature of sadness: learn how to normalize, manage, and reconcile this emotion.

Exercise:

Ask the children to search the Internet for paintings by well-known artists that reflect sadness and the emotions associated with it, such as crying, despair, grief, and shame.

The children will print out the artwork they like the most and post them on the classroom walls. Then they create three sets of cards that include: the artist's name, the painting's title, and a few interesting facts about their chosen painting.

The title cards are placed into one box, and the artist names in another.

Each participant draws a title card and places it beside what they think is the corresponding painting (if they draw their own card, they return it to the box and take another). Repeat this exercise with the artist cards.

Once all the cards have been taken, participants take turns placing their own cards next to the correct painting and reading aloud the interesting facts they wrote on the third card.

With a show of hands, they choose the painting that they think best expresses sadness.

✸ Reflecting on this exercise

- How would you define sadness?
- If sadness was an atmospheric phenomena, which would it be?
- Do tears always comes with sadness?
- Why is it that sometimes you cry and sometimes you don't?
- When you cry, do you feel better or worse?
- Are there any umbrellas that can protect you from an emotional tempest?
- What was the saddest moment in your life?
- What do you do to make yourself feel better when you are sad?
- What can you do to console someone who is sad?

✸ Conclusions and other considerations

Sadness is a basic, normal, and necessary emotion. It manifests when we have lost something in our lives. For some time afterward (long or short), we don't feel like doing much at all.

We must allow ourselves to feel sadness, and it is important not to prevent others from feeling it, too. Saying "don't be sad" doesn't help anyone who feels sad. It is better to say, "Is there anything I can do to make you feel better?" and stay close by.

If we accept sadness instead of repressing it, and remember that when we experience any loss we must allow ourselves a suitable period of mourning, one fine day we will see that time has healed us, and the "sun" will shine again.

SONGS TO WEATHER THE STORM

✿ Objective:

Learn to put on a brave face in bad weather, using music as a strategy to improve your state of mind.

Exercise:

Ask each participant to choose a song or singer that cheers them up and improves their state of mind whenever they feel disheartened or sad, or when things are not going as well as they would like. They should bring a recording of one song to share with the rest of the group.

Sitting in a circle, they take turns presenting their song, explaining why it cheers them up. The group listens to it and assesses whether it has improved their energy levels.

After the session, they can make a list of these songs, titled "Songs to Weather the Storm."

The group might also analyze the messages relayed through the lyrics. It would be useful to distribute printed copies of the lyrics as well.

◉ Reflecting on this exercise

- Why do you think music alters our state of mind? You could research this on the Internet.

- What different emotions can music evoke? Do you think it would be easy to find music that makes you feel sad, or enthusiastic, or annoys you?

- Do you ever use music to change your state of mind?

- Was it difficult to find music that motivates you?

- Did you focus solely on the song's melody or did you also listen to the lyrics?

- What do you think of the music your companions chose?

- How did you feel before, during, and after listening to each song?

◉ Conclusions and other considerations

Sometimes, for no apparent reason, we can lose our get-up-and-go, as if the day suddenly became overcast and approaching black clouds indicate that there will soon be a storm. This can cause our spirits to sink.

It is easy to mistake low spirits for sadness. It is normal to feel this way sometimes, but it's important that we learn to deal with and manage these moments so they do not swamp us with their gray tones and dullness.

There is a well-known saying: "He who sings frightens away his ills." It is important to remember that music, and specifically the act of singing, can help us reconnect with the positive energy that we always carry inside us.

Self-control and self-motivation can help us improve emotional climate.

ALL-WEATHER BAGGAGE

❊ Objective:

To understand that a positive outlook and optimism are the best baggage to pack when traveling to any kind of climate, and only we can decide to take them with us.

Narrative:

The traveler asked the shepherd:
"What will the weather be like today?"
"Just how I like it," came the reply.
"How do you know that it will be just as you like it?"
"Now that I have discovered that I cannot always have what I want, I have learned to be grateful for what I receive. That is why I am sure the weather will be perfect for me today."

After reading this narrative out loud, distribute printed versions to each group member, who will reflect on its contents in silence.

Then distribute a worksheet with images of different weather symbols on it: rain, sun, wind, snow, cold, hot, high humidity, fog, etc.

Ask them to consider only the positive aspects of each phenomenon. For example, rain cools and clears the air, supplements our water supply, irrigates farmland, replenishes aquifers, and forms puddles to play in.

The children then relate each weather phenomenon to one or a number of emotions, considering how they can personally benefit from the positive aspects associated with each phenomenon. For example, if their "climate" is cold and they are alone, they could use this condition to explore themselves further, quietly reflect, concentrate on their work, learn to appreciate the company of others, etc.

❈ Reflecting on this narrative

- Can you always get what you want?

- How do you react when you don't? Do you become angry, resign yourself to it, or look for positives?

- Do you think it is almost always possible to find something good or positive in a difficult situation?

- Can you think of a situation in which you have done this?

- What do you think about the shepherd's strategy? Is it a good way to bring more happiness into your life?

❈ Conclusions and other considerations

Nobody will ask us what kind of weather we want every day. It would be impossible for all of us to agree. That's why the weather surprises us. All we can do is prepare for it by dressing accordingly, so that we have the best possible day.

We need to do something similar in our emotional world. We cannot choose the different situations we are going to experience each day. People surprise us by doing unexpected things and our inner landscape changes its emotional colors. But we can still prepare ourselves before we leave home, gathering up our positive outlook as baggage that will prove helpful to us, no matter what the weather.

KIT FOR EMOTIONALLY INCLEMENT WEATHER

⚙ Objective:

Recognize the different ways we can protect ourselves against "emotional inclemency."

Exercise:

Form three teams of investigators who will present their findings in a bid to win the Innovations in Emotional Development prize. Each team must prepare a "protection against inclement emotions kit" comprising everything that can be useful to prevent or avoid unnecessary suffering in emotionally demanding situations. They will draw up a plan, prepare an instruction sheet explaining the purpose of each component, how they should be used, any known contraindications, etc.

A spokesperson from each team offers their ideas to the group. After everyone has presented, the participants write down the three components they liked the most. These collective items will go into the "protection against inclement emotions kit."

⚙ Reflecting on this exercise

- What is a lightning rod? How could you make use of an emotional lightning rod?

- Could you make the same comparison using other things we use to protect ourselves from inclement weather? For example, sunglasses, sunscreen, a raincoat, umbrella, parasol, boots, hat?

- Which kit components do you already own?

- Of those you don't own, which do you think would prove very useful in emotionally demanding situations?

- Do you have an emotional umbrella to protect you from acid rain?

- What happens when you are exposed to anger, resentment, envy, or insults without any kind of protection?

- Do you think protecting yourself is the same as defending yourself? What are the differences?

⚙ Conclusions and other considerations

We can't control how others manage their chaotic emotions. However, we must learn how to manage our own difficult emotions so that we do not harm ourselves or others. Although we are not responsible for what we feel, we are responsible for our own behavior.

It is also our responsibility to protect ourselves from violence and emotional toxicity. In the same way that we do not expose ourselves to UV radiation from the sun without protecting our skin, or travel to very cold places without winter clothes, we must also take precautions so that we do not suffer unnecessarily from others' emotional garbage.

Positive-outlook glasses, an anti-anger lightning rod, a self-esteem umbrella, and other objects offer us the emotional protection we need to achieve this.

CONTAMINATED PLANETS

- WHAT DO YOU KNOW ABOUT CONTAMINATION?
- HOW DO YOU THINK WE CONTAMINATE?
- DID YOU KNOW THAT WE CAN ALSO CONTAMINATE WITH EMOTIONS?

?

17

Planet Earth is our home, the place we live. It gives us everything we need to survive: water, food, air, our own space, and many other resources. The Earth is very generous!

We share our "home" with other living beings: plants, animals, and humans. How do we relate to them and to the Earth? Do you think we care for our planet as it deserves?

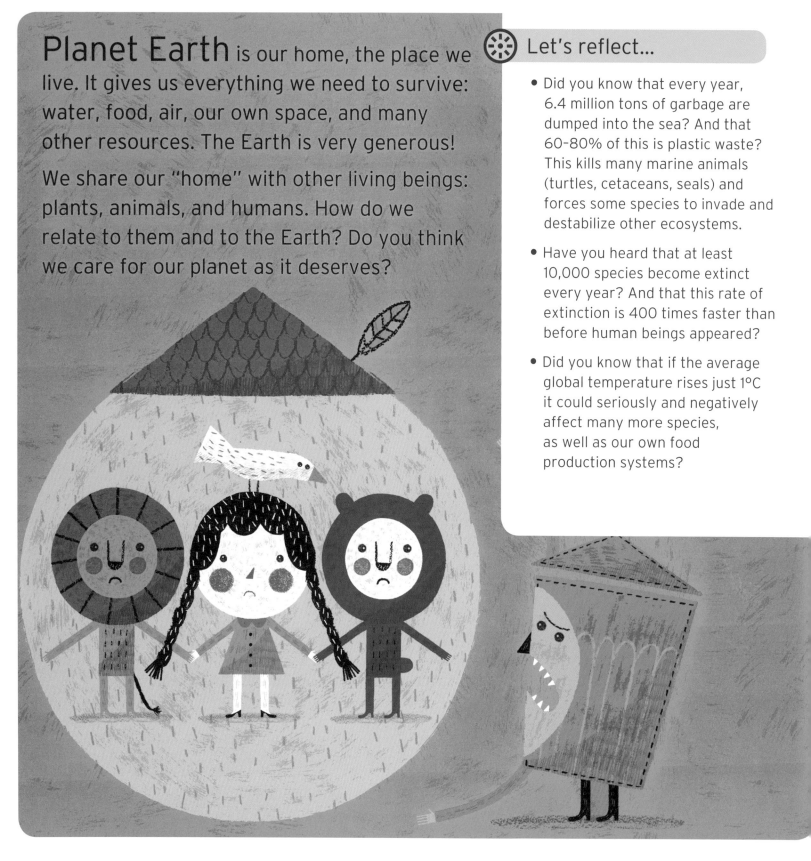

Let's reflect...

- Did you know that every year, 6.4 million tons of garbage are dumped into the sea? And that 60-80% of this is plastic waste? This kills many marine animals (turtles, cetaceans, seals) and forces some species to invade and destabilize other ecosystems.

- Have you heard that at least 10,000 species become extinct every year? And that this rate of extinction is 400 times faster than before human beings appeared?

- Did you know that if the average global temperature rises just 1ºC it could seriously and negatively affect many more species, as well as our own food production systems?

So what's happening on our "inner planet?" Sometimes things make us feel bad. Every day we bottle up anger, rage, envy, and humiliation inside of us without knowing what to do with them. Without realizing it, we become an emotional landfill; we lose our good humor, stop caring for others, and become angry with ourselves and the whole world!

✳ Let's reflect...

- How many times have we been too hard on ourselves or even disrespected ourselves?

- Despite knowing that this does not help us, why do we sometimes keep on behaving the same way instead of doing something to make ourselves feel better?

- Do you ever dump your bad moods on the people around you?

- Why do we let others' opinions hurt us like darts?

- Insults, contempt, mistreatment, and disrespect toward ourselves and others become, over time, emotional waste that impoverishes our lives and jeopardizes our happiness.

WHO DECIDES HOW I MUST BE?

✲ Objective:

To become aware that every one of us can and should choose how we behave around others.

Situation:

I went to the newsstand with my friend Alex to buy a paper. Alex greeted the vendor in a friendly way. However, the vendor responded rudely and thoughtlessly, almost throwing the newspaper toward him. But my friend just kept smiling, calmly paid for his newspaper, and wished the newsagent a good weekend. As we went on our way, I said:

"Is that man always that rude to you?"

"Yes, I'm afraid so," Alex replied.

"And you are always polite and friendly to him?"

"Yes, I am... because

_____."

(Complete the phrase)

✸ Reflecting on this situation

- Why do you think Alex is so friendly toward the vendor?

- How does he do this? What skills and strategies could you use to achieve this?

- Why do you think the vendor is always so unfriendly to Alex?

- Would Alex benefit if he responded to the vendor's negativity with his own?

- How do you think the vendor treats his other customers?

- Do you think someone who is usually grumpy is a happy person?

- How would you have behaved in Alex's place?

✸ Conclusions and other considerations

Every one of us can decide what kind of person we wish to be and not let the behavior of others make that decision for us.

Alex is very sure that he does not want the vendor to influence his behavior; he doesn't want to be an aggressive person. He has chosen to be polite, peaceful, and kind, whatever the emotional climate of those who cross his path.

We can all choose between creation and destruction. We are responsible for our personalities. Depending on our behavior, there will be joy and happiness in our lives, or unpleasantness and unhappiness.

CREATIVE TRASH

⚙ Objective:

Learn that even items we find in the trashcan can help us if
we know how to use them correctly.

Exercise:

Children are asked to bring junk items or pieces of trash from home over the course of a
week, and place them in labeled boxes.

On the last collection day, form teams and ask each team to create something with their
trash. Each team is free to create whatever they can imagine and give their work a title.
Each team should then carefully observe what the others have built and write their
impressions on a sheet of paper: what they think of it, if they like it, what they think it could
be useful for, etc. Each team should explain to the others what it has built and what it is
used for, and then write down any feedback from the other groups.

⚙ Reflecting on this exercise

- What was each object that you brought
  originally used for?

- What is it used for now? Is it still trash?

- Which factors did you consider during
  the transformation?

- Do you think you can do the same with
  feelings and emotions?

- Could you also transform these feelings
  and emotions?

- Which tools would you use to achieve this?

- Is garbage simply junk or can it be something else?

- How did creating something in a group make
  you feel?

⚙ Conclusions and other considerations

While some materials must be safely disposed
of because they are toxic, other items among
our trash can be recycled and transformed. This
is also the case with our emotions. Imagination,
resolution, hard work, and creativity are of great
value to us as we seek to purify our emotional
waste. If we do not want our garbage to become
toxic, we must practice daily "emotional hygiene,"
eliminating what needs to be eliminated, changing
what we are able to change, and working toward
improving the things that can harm us. In this
sense it is important to be open to the sincere
and respectful opinions of those around us who
can help us become better people. Conversely, we
should not listen to those who try to make us feel
bad, considering their opinions as no more than
rubbish that we can do without.

WHAT A DELUGE!

⚙ Objective:

To be aware that some people dump their anger, fear, tension, and hostility on others as if they were trash. This constitutes aggressive behavior and a lack of respect, and they have no right to behave like this.

Situation:

Children are playing soccer in the schoolyard when a player, Maria, stumbles over a stone, unintentionally pushing Marco, who falls to the ground and loses possession of the ball. Marco's team is losing the game, as is often the case.

Marco angrily turns on Maria, shouting at her in front of their friends:

"You're useless! Look what you've done! I fell and lost the ball because of you! You're no good at all. I don't know why we let you play with us. You're always getting in the way. You don't even know how to play soccer. Why don't you go away and play something else? You've got something against me, and you pushed me on purpose. Playing with you is the worst! I'm not going to continue playing if you keep doing this!"

⚙ Reflecting on this situation

- Do you think that what happened was Maria's fault?
- Why do you think that Marco reacted in this way?
- How do you think Maria felt after Marco had "deluged" her with his emotional trash?
- Classify the different types of emotional trash that Marco dumped on Maria.
- Do you think Maria deserved how Marco treated her?
- What can Maria do in this situation?
- If you found yourself in Maria's situation, would you play soccer in the schoolyard again?
- Have you ever experienced something similar? Can you share this experience?
- How would you have reacted if you were Marco?

⚙ Conclusions and other considerations

Emotional pollutants are a reality in our day-to-day life. There are people who hurt, attack, and disregard the feelings of others, sometimes consciously, but sometimes carried away by their own anger or emotional distress. There's no doubt that when these people cross our path, their words can make us feel very bad inside.

It is extremely important that we know how to defend ourselves against insults and disrespect. We should always carry a big self-esteem umbrella to help us achieve this.

But be careful! Every one of us has the potential to become an emotional contaminator. Don't lower your guard!

BUILDING BRIDGES

✦ Objective:

To recognize that words can be powerful. They can form bridges that link us together or be used as missiles to cause harm.

Exercise:

Ask the group to save cardboard tubes from the toilet paper and paper towel rolls they use at home and bring them to class. Once they have gathered a fair number, they will cut them in half horizontally and paint them (they should all be different).

On each halved roll, they will write "missile" words or phrases (that harm the recipient), as well as the context in which they are used.

Then ask the group to build different types of houses from small cardboard boxes.

When everything is ready, try the following activity:

The group's mission is to reconnect two villages that have been totally cut off from each other by torrential rain. The only way to reach one village from the other is to rebuild the bridge between them. But this is a special mission, as the new bridge can't just be any bridge; it can only be built after the missile words or phrases are transformed into "bridge" words or phrases that bring people closer together or improve relationships. Each time the group substitutes a missile half-roll for a bridge half-roll, it can be used to construct the bridge between the two cardboard villages.

Example:

Missile phrase: "You're useless!"

Bridge phrase: "I'm sure you can do better. Can I help?"

◉ Reflecting on this exercise

- How do you think the recipients of each of these missiles felt? How do you think the person who received these missiles would have felt in each situation? And how would they have felt if they had received your bridge words instead?

- Bridge phrases make us more emotionally ecological. Do you use them often?

- Can you think of any famous people known for their use of these bridges?

- What did it mean to you to finally connect the two villages despite the difficulties you faced?

◉ Conclusions and other considerations

When we want to, we can build real bridges that bring us closer to others and show the best of ourselves. The test: we managed to unite two villages that were supposedly completely isolated from each other. This is the goal of bridge words or phrases: to bring our minds, hearts, and souls closer together. Can you put this into practice?

RADIATION LEAK!

⊛ Objective:

To be aware that some emotions are highly toxic and should be disposed of under the strictest conditions of safety and security, protecting both ourselves and those around us from harm.

Situation:

Jorge has been overweight since he was a little boy. Over the years he has put up with taunts from classmates and consequently feels neglected and marginalized. He hasn't learned to respect himself; his strategy has always been to be alone and avoid making emotional connections with those around him. This year he started at a new school. From the very first day he noticed that his new classmates were always looking at him and talking about him behind his back. He didn't want a repeat of what happened in his old school, so he said to them:

"What's wrong? Have you never seen a fat person before? Sit down at your desks and leave me in peace. You're all the same!"

⊛ Reflecting on this situation

- How has Jorge been reacting to his classmates' comments for many years?

- Do you think Jorge is "contaminated"? Why?

- Do you think his new classmates will view him differently?

- Has Jorge started at his new school on the right foot?

- Do you think Jorge loves himself and has a good self-image? Why or why not?

- What measures could Jorge have taken so that he didn't explode in this way? Have you ever exploded in a similar manner?

- What might be the consequences of such behavior?

⊛ Conclusions and other considerations

Just as radioactive waste should be handled with the utmost care, so we must be careful with unpleasant or painful emotions we have accumulated over time. They can end up transforming into highly polluting and toxic emotions that will at some point erupt from inside us in an explosive way.

To avoid dangerous emotional leaks, we must be very careful every time we find ourselves in a risky situation, learning to use our best qualities to protect ourselves. We all have them, it's just a question of looking! Inside each of us are hidden treasures that make us especially valuable – but we must discover them first. We are not merely how much we weigh, how tall we are, the color of our eyes, or the shape of our body – we are so much more.

It is vital that we distance ourselves from impulsive behavior, generalizations, and unpleasant language. To control a leak in time, we need to be able to redirect it in a difficult situation.

MY EMOTIONS ARE JUST LIKE THAT

❁ Objective:

Learn to recognize our emotions and identify the situations, people, and feelings that have caused them and how to better express them.

Exercise:

Ask the class to think about emotions they have felt, write them down on colored pieces of paper, and drop them in a box. Each group will pick out a paper with an emotion written on it. Over the next week they will gather information about this emotion and then present their findings to the rest of the class.

Give them the following guide:

- Look for photographs and pictures that seem to reflect this emotion.
- If this emotion was a color, which color would it be?
- Look for other words (synonyms) that convey this emotion.
- Draw a picture about this emotion.
- Take a photograph in which they express this emotion.
- What happens to our bodies when we experience this emotion?
- Which feelings and facial expressions are associated with this emotion?
- In what kind of situations does it typically occur?
- Make a mime of the emotion and present it to the class.

❁ Reflecting on this exercise

- Did all group members agree on how to express this emotion? Are our thoughts, body language, and the way we express it the same for each of us?

- Were some group members better mimes than others?

- Did you all agree as you were selecting your images, or were there differences in opinion?

- Which emotions do you think are the easiest to perceive? The most difficult?

❁ Conclusions and other considerations

At one time or another, we have all felt the emotions we've been studying. The more information we have about an emotion, the quicker we can identify it in ourselves and the people around us.

Being more aware of the emotions that hurt us means that we can take measures to manage them and prevent them from becoming toxic. Expressing them in a timely and appropriate way is a good start. We can do this in a number of ways: through words, images, facial expressions, and drawings.

Remember that the same emotion can have a different expression and meaning for each person.

TSUNAMIS

- WHAT IS A TSUNAMI?
- HOW IS IT TRIGGERED?
- DID YOU KNOW THAT IF WE GET CARRIED AWAY WITH OUR ANGER, WE CAN BECOME AN "EMOTIONAL TSUNAMI"?

?

29

Tsunami is a Japanese word. *Tsu* means port or bay, and *-nami* means wave. A tsunami is a wave or series of waves produced when enormous forces under the sea result in a huge displacement of water.

Tsunamis are incredibly destructive. They generate such a massive body of fast-moving water that they are powerful enough to wash away houses and kill animals and people with the debris they accumulate. Disease, polluted drinking water, and food shortages follow a disaster of this magnitude.

 Let's reflect...

- Did you know that tsunamis can be triggered by earthquakes or tremors, volcanoes, meteorites, and huge explosions?

- Did you know that the biggest tsunami on record occured in 1883, when the volcano Krakatoa erupted and produced waves up to 138 feet high that devastated the islands of Java and Sumatra?

- Did you know that the waves produced by a tsunami can reach up to sixty-two miles wide on the open ocean? That's the equivalent of 1,000 football fields end-to-end!

All the energy we create but do not carefully manage becomes destructive energy. When we have a problem, we must look for a peaceful solution rather than getting carried away with our anger. The accumulated energy of negative emotions such as anger, rage, resentment, jealousy, or malice can cause dangerous emotional tsunamis. If we let these emotions get out of control, we can become destructive and harmful individuals. For this reason, we must learn to channel our emotional energy more ecologically. Instead of breaking, we must mold; instead of screaming, sing; instead of fighting, exercise; instead of complaining, we must look for solutions to our problems.

Aristotle once said, "Anyone can become angry; that is easy. But to be angry with the right person at the right moment for the right purpose and to the right degree, that is not within everyone's power and is not easy." His words show us how to avoid emotional tsunamis.

✳ Let's reflect...

- Have you ever become angry at your friends but taken it out on your family members at home?

- Have you ever been carried away by your anger, shouting insults until you felt better? Do you think that this is a good way to fix something?

- Do you think you can express your anger without behaving aggressively toward those around you? How?

- Did you know that you can learn to redirect energy created by anger so that it transforms into energy that makes us better people?

HOW CAN WE **IMPROVE** OUR SELF-CONTROL?

WHEN ENVY TAKES CONTROL

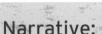 **Objective:**

To learn that if we let our envy get out of control, we can destroy or damage those around us, and that envy is a sure sign that there is something we must improve in ourselves.

Narrative:

Legend has it that a snake began to chase a firefly. The terrified firefly tried to escape, but the snake wasn't going to quit that easily. It chased the firefly for the entire day, and then into a second day, refusing to give up its pursuit. On the third day, the exhausted firefly finally came to a stop and said to the serpent:

"May I ask you three questions?"

"I wouldn't usually agree to such a request, but as I'm going to eat you anyway, you can ask me what you like," the serpent responded.

"Do you consider fireflies your natural prey?"

"No," conceded the snake.

"And have I ever done anything to hurt you?"

"I suppose not."

"Then why is it that you want me dead?"

"Because I can't bear to see how much you shine," the snake was forced to admit.

Reflecting on this narrative

- Why do you think the serpent was chasing the firefly?
- Which characteristic of the firefly made the snake envious?
- Has something attractive in a person ever made you envious? How did you react?
- Did you know that each of us has valuable qualities and characteristics? Have you discovered what yours are yet?
- Do you think the snake would have acted the same way if it valued its beautiful skin, its speed, and the elegance with which it glides across the ground?

Conclusions and other considerations

Envy is a mirror that can reflect our perceived inadequacies. When we look into the mirror, we see that others have more than we do, or are better than we are, and this makes us feel frustrated.

It is normal to feel envious. But the more comfortable we feel in ourselves, the less likely we are to experience this emotion.

Envy is a sign that something needs to be improved, and we should take the opportunity to ask ourselves: "What makes me envious toward this person? Their good looks? Then I will search for the beauty inside me and improve the characteristics I have neglected. Or perhaps their intelligence? Then I will try harder to learn and study more."

If we respond in this way, we will become better people and part of the solution instead of part of the problem.

CREATE AND DESTROY

⚙ Objective:

To be aware that destruction is quick and easy, while creation is a more gradual and gratifying process that requires a combination of singular components: ideas, time, effort, communication, creativity, and imagination.

Exercise:

In this exercise the group will shoot a video for review and reflection.

Lay out the following materials on a table: magazines, newspapers, cardboard tubes, sticks that have fallen from trees, inflated balloons, washable paints, etc. Tell the class that when the music plays (high-tempo music with a drum beat, the noisier the better) they can destroy, break, and stamp on everything they want to.

When the music stops, they must sit. Ask them to remain silent, close their eyes, and breathe deeply.

Then ask them to open their eyes and look around. What do they think about the state the classroom is in? Do they like it? How does it make them feel?

Next play some pleasant, slow-tempo music and ask them to make something with the things they have destroyed – perhaps a sculpture or something else that is creative, beautiful, or useful. This can be done individually or in groups. Prepare a table with glue, tape, a stapler, water, sponges, and spray paint and allow the students half an hour to complete the task. Give each individual or group a large tag on which to write the title of their works of art.

⚙ Reflecting on this exercise

- Which process was quicker: destruction or creation?

- Which was easier?

- How did you feel during the first part of the exercise? How about the second?

- Do you think something new and better can be created from something that has been destroyed?

- What must we do to accomplish this?

- Which personal qualities did you have to use to achieve this?

⚙ Conclusions and other considerations

Sometimes we must destroy something bad to create something better in its place. But destruction for the sake of destruction is a dangerous strategy.

To create something we must imagine it, dream it, and be prepared to dedicate time and energy to making it a reality. It could take a long time and require patience, but it will eventually bring us happiness and emotional well-being.

Destruction is quick and easy and seems like a good way to vent our anger. However, we can become unbalanced and insensitive, shutting valuable assets and individuals out of our lives.

SOW ANGER, SOW PEACE

✸ Objective:

To be aware that we can choose which emotional "species" to sow and grow inside us. Learn how much better it is to cultivate peace than anger.

Exercise:

The class divides into five groups and sows the seeds of two different plants in the same rectangular flowerpot. One of the plants will be designated the "angry" plant, and the other the "peaceful" plant. Initially each plant is assigned an equal half of the pot. The group must then decide on a strategy following these rules: they can only sow one seed of one of the plants, but several of the other, caring for them as they start to grow. But then they must choose to look after just one or both of the plants, with each group keeping an observation journal recording such things as how they are nourished, whether they have been cut back, whether they've grown to an excessive size, whether they're left alone, etc. After a length of time that allows the class to observe how their plants mature and develop, each group writes up their conclusions.

✸ Reflecting on this exercise

- What did you think about this activity? How did you feel while you were doing it?

- What is the most important thing you learned?

- Have you learned any lessons that can be applied to your everyday lives?

- What do you think would have happenned if you had made different strategy decisions in the care of your plants?

- What can we do to ensure that a peaceful plant occupies more space than an angry plant growing inside us?

✸ Conclusions and other considerations

Every day we decide which emotional species to grow inside of us and then feed them with vitamins and fertilizer. Anger and peace cannot grow together; as one of them grows, the other recedes because they share the same emotional habitat.

We feed our anger when we perceive others as our enemies and compete against them, thinking of them as obstacles to what we want to achieve; and when we let our emotions dictate our behavior, forget that we are not the only ones with objectives and dreams, act selfishly, or are unhelpful and demanding.

We fertilize our inner peace when we work patiently, perceive those around us as collaborators or allies, work as a team, control our emotions, share our goals and help others achieve theirs, are generous, and seek peaceful solutions rather than conflict.

MY PRIMITIVE SIDE

Objective:

To be aware that we all have a "primitive side" living within us that generates selfishness through our survival instincts.

Exercise:

Prepare a collection of animated movie or TV clips that portray characters screaming, hitting, insulting, hoarding, cheating, breaking things, forcing the other characters to do something they don't want to, etc. Watch this with the group.

Give each child a piece of paper and ask them to make a list of selfish, unhelpful, or destructive behaviors they observed while watching the cartoons.

Once they have completed their lists, divide them into groups of five to compile a shared list. They should jot down how each character must have felt to be targeted by each type of behavior. For example, if they were shouted at, they might feel sad, scared, or angry.

Finally, each student draws a picture that represents their primitive side and a second picture that represents their rational side. Hang these pictures on the classroom wall and discuss them with the group.

Reflecting on this exercise

- What did you think about this activity? How did you feel while you were doing it?

- What is the most important thing you learned?

- Have you learned any lessons that can be applied to your everyday lives?

- What do you think would have happened if you had made different strategy decisions in the care of your plants?

- What can we do to ensure that a peaceful plant occupies more space than an angry plant growing inside us?

Conclusions and other considerations

The human brain is made up of different areas that have evolved over a long period of time: The Reptilian Brain is responsible for our vital functions: breathing, moving, preserving our body temperature. The Limbic or Emotional Brain regulates our basic emotions, protecting us and allowing us to react quickly to danger; for example, fear makes us attack, flee, or protect ourselves, and anger gives us strength to remove obstacles. The Rational Brain allows us to reflect, analyze, consider the consequences of our actions, and make voluntary decisions. While we should not ignore the signals that the Reptilian and Emotional Brains are sending us, it is the Rational Brain that we should rely on to govern our lives and decide how to behave.

SCARS OF ANGER

⚙ Objective:

To realize that getting carried away with anger has consequences for both us and those around us.

Narrative:

Martin was always a bit grumpy. When he became annoyed, he would let his anger get the better of him and say and do things that hurt people close to him. Eventually his father gave him a bag of nails and told him to hammer one into his bedroom door every time he felt angry. After that first day he counted thirty-seven nails! Over the following weeks, the number decreased every day; little by little Martin was realizing that it was easier to control his anger than drive nails into his solid wood door. The day finally came when he didn't use any nails. His father then suggested that he remove one nail every day he didn't feel angry. Time passed, and one day Martin told his father that he had taken out all the nails. They sat down together in his bedroom and his father said:

"You've done very well, Martin, but look at all the holes you have made in your door. When a person cannot control their anger, they cause scars like these. A verbal injury can be just as painful as a physical injury. Anger always leaves its mark. Never forget that!"

⚙ Reflecting on this narrative

- What happened to Martin?

- Have you ever behaved like Martin?

- How did you feel afterward? How do you think the people felt who were the target of your anger?

- What do you think about this nails-in-the-door strategy? Can you think of any other strategies that would make you aware of when you lose self-control?

- Have you ever felt hurt after being shouted at, insulted, or heard harsh words from an angry person?

- How did you react?

- Why do think we sometimes behave like this?

⚙ Conclusions and other considerations

Anger doesn't just scar the person who is the target. The angry person also suffers from the fallout: others will keep their distance, the angry person's self-esteem will diminish, and he will feel unhappy.

Bottled-up anger that vents of its own accord is called fury. A furious person loses control and can become like a tsunami, damaging everything in his path.

If we do not let out our suppressed anger, it will turn into rage and scar us inside.

It isn't healthy to suppress other emotions, either. It is always better to release them non-aggressively, taking great care how we express ourselves and considering the best way to say what we need to say without hurting anyone. This is why we must calm ourselves before we speak to a person whose behavior has angered us.

AN EMOTIONAL CATASTROPHE

Objective:

To recognize that we can react to situations in unfair, unhelpful, or aggressive ways, and that improving our emotional self-control is essential to avoid this.

Exercise:

Form groups of five children and direct each group to gather information over the course of one week about natural phenomena that result in disasters (volcanic eruptions, hurricanes, earthquakes, tsunamis, wildfires, floods). The children should consider the characteristics of each phenomenon, how, and why it occurs, whether it can be prevented, and how its effects can be minimized. They should also find some pictures for the mural they will create later.

At the end of the week, they should collate the material they have compiled and create their mural.

During this task, they should also consider what might constitute emotional parallels to the natural disasters they have studied. For example: "I am like a volcanic eruption when I . . . My insults are like the rocks that it throws out, while its ash represents . . . The damage I can do is like . . . Those living nearby (react, feel like . . .), etc."

They can also look for articles in newspapers or on the Internet that highlight these comparisons.

Each group then presents what they have discovered and a discussion begins. They should write down their conclusions in a notebook that will serve as a manual explaining how to behave properly in case of an emotional disaster emergency.

Reflecting on this exercise

- Do you see yourself as a volcano, hurricane, or uncontrolled emotional phenomenon, or more as a victim of this type of catastrophe?

- Do you know anyone who behaves like these phenomena?

- If you could prepare a class survival kit to maintain "emotional health" during such natural disasters, what would it consist of?

- Can you compile a list of resources that would help you survive?

Conclusions and other considerations

If we suppress our negative emotions, they will slowly accumulate inside of us and make us tense and irritable. If something unexpected happens or things don't go our way, an internal mechanism can take over, exposing our primitive side to the world. When our primitive side emerges and grows, it takes control of our Rational Brain; as a result we can damage those around us and do other bad things. For this reason we should not suppress our emotions when we take offense, are insulted, jealous, angry, moody, and fractious, or feel powerless or frustrated.

We must practice emotional hygiene every day, quietly cleaning out any accumulated negative residual emotions. We must prepare ourselves differently for a blizzard than a hurricane, rainfall than a flood, tidal surge than a tsunami. Prevention remains the best cure!

ACID
RAIN

- Do you know what **ACID RAIN** is?
- What effect does it have on the **NATURAL WORLD?**
- Did you know that emotional contamination **CAN PRODUCE SOMETHING SIMILAR?**

?

41

Acid rain is one of the consequences of polluted air. Different types of chemicals are released into the atmosphere when fuel is burned. Factory smoke and automobile exhaust do not only consist of visible gray particles, but also many invisible gases that are highly detrimental to our environment.

Power plants, factories, machinery, and cars burn fuels and produce pollutant gases. Some of these gases react on contact with humidity in the air and transform into acids that are eventually deposited in clouds. The rain produced from these clouds is known as acid rain.

✳ Let's reflect...

- Did you know that acid rain consists partly of gases?
- How many forests are destroyed annually by acid rain? Can you research this on the Internet?
- Which other destructive qualities does it have?
- How does its toxicity affect our health?

In our everyday lives

we also release contaminating elements that we leave unprocessed into the atmosphere: complaints, victimization, dissatisfaction, blame, insults, negative criticism, contempt, ill-humor, etc. These occur because we do not properly manage our chaotic emotions: jealousy, envy, fear, hopelessness, frustration, loneliness, sadness.

We are responsible for disposing of our own garbage without harming others. It is a good idea to dedicate a few moments each day to our emotional hygiene. If we don't, we are at risk of using those around us as trashcans, dumping our tension and toxicity over them.

We reap what we sow, and if we don't like what we reap, we should take a closer look at our emissions. Every single emotion has an impact on the world around us and we are required to manage it in a sustainable way. As Gandhi once said, "We arrange our hair every day, so why not our hearts?"

☀ Let's reflect...

- Which three emotions most commonly affect those around us? Are they clean and ecological or toxic? Do they make us feel good or bad?

- Which three emotions do you most frequently emit into the environment?

- Do you think they can cause harm? Or are they sources of happiness and well-being?

Do you own a **SELF-ESTEEM UMBRELLA** sturdy enough to **PROTECT YOURSELF FROM IT?**

IDEAS
TO BUILD SELF ESTEEM

THE TREASURE INSIDE US

✳ Objective:

To recognize how valuable we are and what we carry inside us. Our other aspects are superficial and not nearly as important.

Situation:

The story is told that as Martin Luther King was about to deliver one of his famous speeches about human rights, he noticed a young African American boy at the front of the auditorium. Surprised, he called over one his aides, who informed him that the boy had been one of the first to arrive.

After the speech, multicolored balloons were released, and King noticed that the boy couldn't take his eyes off them. He approached the boy, hugged him, and took him up in his arms.

The boy gazed at him and asked if the black balloons would fly right up to the sky with the others. King regarded him affectionately and replied, "Balloons don't fly skyward because of their color, but what they have inside them."

⚙ Reflecting on this situation

- Do you know who Martin Luther King was? Can you find out more about him?

- What does the phrase "Balloons don't fly skyward because of their color, but what they have inside them" mean to you?

- Do you think how a person looks on the outside is important?

- Do you take time to look at what people are like on the inside?

- Is there any part or characteristic of yourself that you don't like? Why? Is there something that other people don't like? Why?

- How do you feel if someone rejects you?

- How do you feel when others appreciate you?

- Can you make a list of your ten best qualities?

⚙ Conclusions and other considerations

Never before in the history of humanity has there been anyone quite like you. We are all unique, irreplaceable, and valuable.

It is important to appreciate how different we are, using this knowledge to develop together and learn from each other, rather than using it to exclude or reject.

As Saint-Exupéry's Little Prince says: "What is essential is invisible to the eye." Many of the important things in life are not easily perceived. It doesn't make sense to be guided by appearances. It is what we have inside us that enables us to "fly;" it is there that we should look for what we need, rather than considering what is projected by an external image.

Regardless of what others think, we need to recognize the qualities that make us valuable and work to improve them daily.

WATERMELON OR DRAGON?

⚙ Objective:
To learn that when a belief becomes fixed in our minds, it is difficult to disregard or change our preconceptions about it.

Narrative:

A very long time ago, in the distant hills of Patagonia in Argentina, there was a tiny village. Its inhabitants went hungry because they were afraid to cultivate their land; they had seen a fearsome dragon roaming their fields. Then one day two travelers arrived asking for food. The villagers explained that they had nothing to give them because the dragon was preventing them from harvesting their crops.

The travelers wasted no time in offering to slay the beast. But when the first arrived at the spot where the dragon had been seen, he discovered that what had terrified the villagers was in fact not a dragon, but a colossal watermelon! He explained this to the locals, laughing all the while. However, they didn't believe him and became very angry.

The second stranger headed out across the fields toward this giant watermelon, drew his sword, and hacked it into little pieces. He returned to the village and announced: "I have vanquished what you were afraid of."

The villagers crowded the second traveler, hugging him and inviting him to stay awhile and enjoy their hospitality. He lodged with them for many months, certainly enough time to teach them, little by little, the difference between a dragon and a watermelon.

🜨 Reflecting on this narrative

- Do you think sometimes when we see dragons, they are in fact only harmless watermelons? Can you think of an example of something that scared you at first until you realized it was harmless?

- Does it help when someone reassures you that "there's no reason to be scared"? What is it exactly that helps you to feel better? If someone teases you about things you are scared of, how do you feel?

- Which traveler acted with more intelligence? Why?

- Do you see and perceive things the same as other people?

- Why do you think individuals react to identical situations in different ways?

⚛ Conclusions and other considerations

Some people seek to force what they know or have learned on those around them.

Ridiculing and teasing others about their fears does not achieve anything and can damage their self-esteem.

We are not always receptive to new information; when we damage someone else's self-esteem, we can drive them away from us. Each and every person requires time to accept new concepts, and it is important that we respect this process.

We must be very careful when we express our "truths."

AN EMOTIONAL UMBRELLA

❋ Objective:

Understand that self-esteem can be a sturdy umbrella protecting us from the damage that others around us can inflict (insults, contempt, etc.).

Exercise:

Ask each child to look for an old, unusable umbrella. Explain that the umbrella metaphorically represents their self-esteem. The first part of this exercise involves naming the individual ribs, selecting names that reflect a substance, quality, or value that is necessary to build self-esteem: confidence, respect, self-knowledge, bravery, assertiveness, friendliness, happiness, optimism, positive experiences, affection, persistence.

It is vital that each class member comes up with these names by themselves. If they struggle, the teacher can prepare a small box of colored cards with appropriate names written on them. The children then draw these cards until they find names that they recognize as important to their own self-esteem.

These cards should then be hung from the bottom of each rib with fishing line. To conclude this part of the exercise, the supervisor distributes another set of cards on which the students write actions or processes that improve the quality hanging from the bottom of the corresponding rib (examples for confidence might include: tell myself "no problem" when things go wrong and try again, be brave enough to try new things, remember my ten best qualities). Then they attach these new cards to the top of the umbrella ribs, near the center.

The children then decorate their umbrella as they like before presenting it to the rest of the group.

❋ Reflecting on this exercise

- What was the most difficult part of this exercise? Why?

- What was the easiest part?

- Did any of your classmates help you to recognize personal characteristics in yourself?

- Are you reassured to know that you could hang an emotional umbrella in the room to shelter you from the acid rain produced by your classmates?

❋ Conclusions and other considerations

Our self-esteem grows as we realize we are worthy of love and respect and are of great value. To properly cultivate our self-esteem we must first take into account our characteristics, competencies, and potential; we must work to improve these every day.

The ignorance that surrounds us can make us feel insecure.

Throughout our lives we will meet toxic individuals that can breach even the sturdiest emotional umbrella. When this happens it is best to have nothing more to do with them, choosing instead to associate with healthy and respectful people. It is important to look after our beautiful umbrellas and continue to reinforce them. We shouldn't let anyone dump their trash over our heads!

THE UGLY DUCKLING

Objective:

Become conscious that "emotional acid rain" is a common phenomenon that can anger us and make us suffer. Analyze the emotions and behavior that cause this phenomenon and look for more respectful ways to communicate with those around us.

Situation:

Hand each participant a worksheet with the following text:

The others went out of their way to harass the ugly duckling as much as they possibly could. They swooped down on him, biting, pecking, hissing, and screeching. They treated him ever more badly as time passed. The duckling hid, or zigzagged from right to left as he tried to dodge them . . . but he could not escape.

He became the most miserable creature that had ever lived in this world.

Hans Christian Andersen, *The Ugly Duckling* (excerpt)

Ask each pupil to consider how the ugly duckling must have felt to suffer this abuse.

Then ask them to think of positive responses to the negative comments below:

How might you respond if someone said to you . . . "You're weird."

"You're ugly/unattractive."

"I don't know which rock you crawled out from under."

"It would be better if you had never been born."

"Things would be much better if you weren't here."

"You are the reason we are unhappy."

"You're no use for anything."

"You make our lives more difficult."

"There's no helping you."

"It's all your fault."

"Don't even bother trying, surely you'll fail."

"You'll never be able to do that."

In groups of five, consider how we can neutralize this acid rain of cruel words. What you discover will become your "umbrellas" that protect you from contamination.

Reflecting on this situation

- Which insults or comments hurt you the most? Can you make a list?

- How did they make you feel?

- Do you ever hurl insults or shower acid rain on those around you?

- How do you think others feel when you do this?

- Do you think you can reduce the levels of acid rain you cause or receive?

- What can we do to better protect ourselves against those who cause acid rain?

Conclusions and other considerations

We are brave and respectful beings. We should never stop being ourselves in order to be accepted by someone else.

When others treat us badly we have four clear courses of action: attack, surrender, retreat, or reinforce our personal resources, protecting ourselves and continuing to grow and develop.

We must be clear about who we are and not become the first "name" someone gives us. A wise African proverb says: "It is not a matter of what someone calls you, but how you respond. However, if you do not know who you are, anyone can give you a name and thereafter you will respond to any name."

A SACK FULL OF "AWFUL"

✺ Objective:

To learn how to manage the emotional ecology of our chaotic emotions. Understand that while it is impossible to avoid an "awful," it is vital that we fully understand it so that we can manage it better.

Exercise:

Each participant compiles a list of the emotions they feel during an "awful." This list should be as exhaustive as possible. To make this task easier for them, pin a list of chaotic and unpleasant emotions on the classroom wall.

Accompanied by music, each child writes their name and "sack full of awful" on a label and puts it on a trash bag. Then they make a sticker with a chaotic emotion that they feel during an "awful" and put it on old newspaper they've crumpled into balls. They should continue to do this until they have as many labeled paper balls as emotions on their lists.

Finally they place all the balls inside the trash bag and close it with tape. The sacks are placed in a line and the children sit in a large circle around them. They stand one at a time and disclose the contents of their sack, saying: "My awful sack contains loneliness, fear, rage, injustice, frustration, sadness, sorrow, envy . . ." As they call out each emotion, they will extract the corresponding ball from their sack and toss it to one side. When all of the participants have emptied their sacks, the classroom will be full of paper balls. The teacher can assign groups to collect different types of emotional balls and assess the best way to dispose of them.

⚙ Reflecting on this exercise

- Did you notice if your "awful" sack contained the same emotions as your classmates'?
- Did this exercise make you experience any emotions you have never felt before?
- Which emotion was most commonly found in the sacks? Why do you think it appeared most frequently?
- Would you prefer a closed-up awful sack or an open one that lets you release what you feel?
- Have you ever felt an "emotional knot" anywhere in your body?
- Have you ever showered anyone with your unpleasant emotions? Or maybe they showered you?
- What do you think you could do so that you don't accumulate so many emotions in your sack?

⚙ Conclusions and other considerations

We are unable to manage an "awful" unless we find out what it consists of. Furthermore, an "awful" consists of different things for each one of us.

We must first allow ourselves to feel chaotic emotions, then recognize and name them, before finally expressing the message we wish to convey.

It is important to express what we feel as soon as we have calmed ourselves down, without letting our emotional waste accumulate over time.

As we become aware of what our "awful sack" contains, we can decide how to safely dispose of its contents: recycle what we can, learn lessons where there are lessons to be learned, and eliminate its toxicity, being careful not to harm those around us. Remember the words of Aristotle and apply them: person, moment, purpose, and degree.

WHOSE PRESENT IS THAT?

Objective:

Realize that while we cannot control how and what others communicate to us, we can decide whether or not we want to be showered by their "acid rain."

Exercise:

Hand each participant a worksheet with the following text: The guru asked them: "If someone comes to you with a present and you do not accept it, who does it belong to?" "To the person who tried to gift it," one of his followers responded. "The same is true for envy, anger, and disrespect," came the guru's reply. "If they are rejected, they remain the property of the one who bears them."

After reading the text out loud, give each participant five sheets of blank paper and five envelopes, on which they will write the names of five other classmates. On each paper they write an opinion they have about the addressee. The messages are placed in their envelopes and the children walk around the classroom while soft music plays. When they come across one of the five addressees, they deliver their envelope. The recipients open and read their messages and choose whether to keep them or return them to the sender. This part of the exercise should be carried out in silence and concludes when all five messages have been delivered (or returned to sender).

To conclude this exercise, the students sit and count how many envelopes they have in their possession and explain in turn why they chose to return some of them to their classmates. The content of any returned message is examined to see how the same opinion could have been expressed without hurting someone else's feelings.

Reflecting on this exercise

- How many of the messages you handed out were returned to you? Why do you think that happened?

- How many of the messages did you return to sender? Can you explain why?

- Was it easy or difficult to return them?

- Do you think we should take into account every single opinion others have of us?

- Why do we sometimes let others shower us with toxic words, showing us a lack of respect?

- What do you think would happen if you said to them, "that's only one way to look at it"?

- How many envelopes did you keep? Why?

Conclusions and other considerations

We have all felt unfairly judged by our classmates, friends, and family at one time or another. This makes us feel miserable, abandoned, lonely, and sad; or perhaps furious, powerless, rejected, and frustrated. Their words and behavior certainly awaken emotions in us that cause us to suffer.

If we can consider that at least a part of their criticism is well-intentioned (even though it may be difficult for us to accept), we will have created our own "early warning system" that helps us take the criticism in stride. Remember: any criticism made with respect is an opportunity for personal growth, although it can seem hurtful at first. However, we must throw any negative or disrespectful criticism directly in the trash and not allow it to awaken any emotions in us.

REDUCE, RECYCLE, REUSE, AND REPAIR

- WHAT DOES **THE WORD "SUSTAINABLE"** MEAN TO YOU?
- WOULD YOU SAY THAT YOUR EMOTIONAL LIFESTYLE IS **SUSTAINABLE OR UNSUSTAINABLE?**
- HAVE YOU EVER HEARD OF THE **4 R'S OF EMOTIONAL SUSTAINABILITY?**

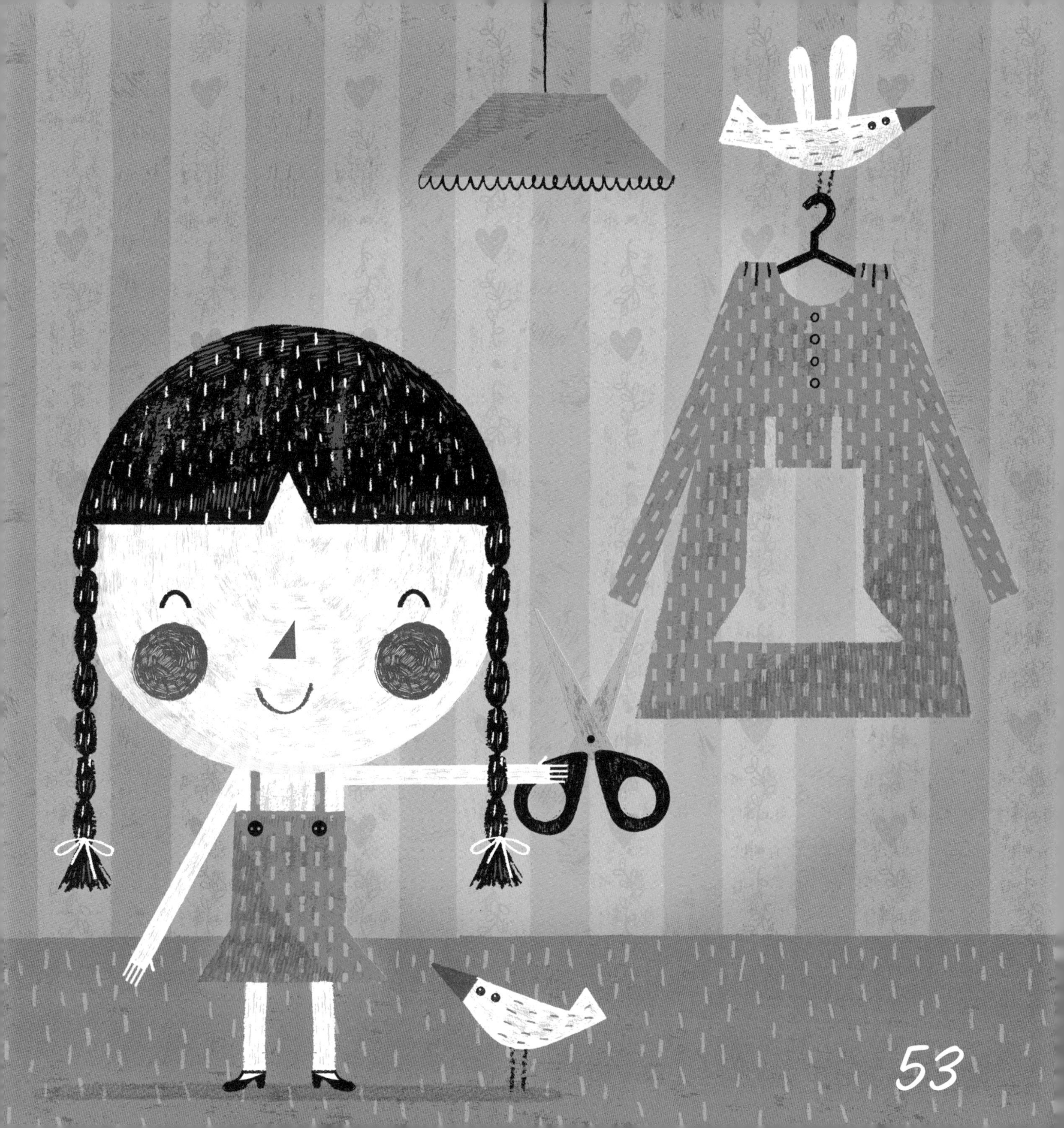

Our forests are a source of life and health, habitats where a huge variety of plants, animals, insects, and people coexist. They produce oxygen and charm us with their beauty, calm, and peace. We must care for them because they are essential to the balance of our world's climate. Indiscriminate tree felling and acid rain are transforming once-thriving ecosystems into desert landscapes. Without trees and their roots to absorb rainfall, fertile soil is washed away. Huge areas become less and less productive and life struggles to gain a foothold. In environmental terms, it would be suicidal to stop caring for our forests. We must reduce their contamination; replenish them when they are weak; maintain paths and throughways; work to eliminate disease and debris; fertilize, protect, prune, replant, clean, recycle, reuse, and repair them, giving them the space to breathe and develop.

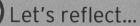

Let's reflect...

- Did you know that 71% of the world's forest habitat has been destroyed over the last twenty years?

- Did you know that when we recycle one ton of paper, we save seventeen trees, 13,000 gallons of water, and more than 80 gallons of petrol?

- Did you know that deforestation is responsible for 20% of greenhouse gases?

- Do you think this is sustainable?

- Do you think you can do anything to save our planet's forests and jungles?

Emotional ecologists should be wise and willing, like trees, to "shed old leaves" from their mind and heart when necessary. They also safely dispose of their daily emotional trash by maintaining their emotional hygiene and applying the four R's: Reduce, Recycle, Reuse, and Repair.

If we do not use these four R's to manage our own natural resources, they too will eventually be exhausted. In the same way, if we stop learning, enjoying ourselves, becoming inspired, dreaming, loving, limiting our creativity, or ceasing to appreciate the wonders around us, we too will be left without "roots." Hopelessness, sadness, apathy, resentment, ill-humor, unhappiness, and a feeling of powerlessness will turn us into "deserts." We must immediately replant and repopulate our hearts with the best possible emotional species!

✳ Let's reflect...

- Which emotions do you think it is important to reduce in our lives?

- Which emotions do you think you can recycle?

- Which qualities do you possess but do not apply, that you could reuse to improve your life?

- Which emotional wounds must you repair or overlook to regain your tranquility and happiness?

DO YOU WANT TO LEARN TO **REDUCE, RECYCLE, REUSE, AND REPAIR** SO THAT YOUR OWN RESOURCES ARE NEVER EXHAUSTED?

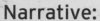

WHICH WOLF WINS?

⚙ Objective:

To bear in mind how important it is to reduce chaotic emotions while dedicating more and more resources to those that contribute towards our wellbeing.

Narrative:

The old tribal chieftain was having an animated discussion with his grandchildren about life. At one point he said to them, "There is a great struggle taking place inside my heart. There are two wolves fighting. One wolf represents evil, fear, anger, jealousy, envy, pain, bitterness, greed, arrogance, guilt, resentment, lies, pride, selfishness, over-ambition, and dominance. The other wolf represents kindness, courage, joy, peace, hope, serenity, humility, gentleness, generosity, tenderness, friendship, truth, compassion, and love.

This same fight is taking place inside every human being that inhabits the Earth."

When he finished, the children were quiet for several minutes, until one of them asked:

"So Grandfather, which wolf wins?" To which the old chieftain replied, "The wolf that wins is the wolf we feed more."

⚙ Reflecting on this narrative

- Which of these two wolves do you think predominates inside of you? Do you think it is possible for someone to only have one of these wolves?

- Does your bad wolf ever win? How does this make you feel?

- What do you think you need to do so that the good wolf wins? How would it make you feel?

- How do you think you can feed the good wolf? And how can you stop the bad wolf from getting any stronger?

- Do you think it is possible to recycle any of the unpleasant emotions the chieftain mentions in his story? How?

⚙ Conclusions and other considerations

We must all learn to live with contrasting tendencies: creativity and destruction, good and evil, life and death. They exist inside all of us and it is vital that we do not repress this fact. However, we can choose which of them we feed and which one we keep well-controlled.

The values that guide us through our lives favor one wolf or another. Generosity, austerity, solidarity, self-control, and gratitude favor the good wolf, while selfishness, wastefulness, individualism, recklessness, and ignorance favor the bad wolf.

We must therefore decide which of our wolves we are going to weaken and which we are going to feed.

WORLD CONGRESS ON SOLVING PROBLEMS

⊕ Objective:

To realize that we often misclassify something that is merely inconvenient as a problem. We must learn to perceive situations in the right context without blowing them out of proportion.

Exercise:

This is an exercise for groups of five participants. The instructions are as follows:

You are journalists who have been brought together to attend the World Congress on Solving Problems. Your mission is to classify these problems, in order of importance, into three categories: problems, difficulties, and inconveniences.

The first part of this exercise is to agree on the criteria for each category. Then each group considers the highest-profile global news stories of the previous week and classifies them into one of the three categories. They'll choose three of these stories to present at the World Congress on Solving Problems.

After everyone has presented, ask for a show of hands to decide the winning group.

Finally, the participants reflect on how these criteria can be applied in their everyday lives. Each participant writes down a problem, difficulty, and inconvenience they encounter in their personal lives.

⊕ Reflecting on this exercise

- Did you feel different when you assessed a situation in one way or another?

- What is the most difficult problem you have ever had to solve?

- Is there any problem in your life that you can't find a solution to?

- Have you ever made one of your inconveniences into a problem?

- Can you suggest a solution for each of the three finalists?

- Do you think that together we can change the world for the better?

⊛ Conclusions and other considerations

Problems, difficulties, and mere inconveniences are very different things.

Every problem has its own solution. We only need to learn to ask the right questions, and we will work out how to deal with them.

When we turn something that seemed to be a problem into an inconvenience, we lessen its emotional impact and feel better.

To reduce tension, toxins, concerns, anxiety, irritability, violence, aggression, resentment, and frustration, we must practice emotional ecology.

MY TREE OF PROBLEMS

✱ Objective:

To recognize that we accumulate problems and worries, both large and small, every day of our lives. They can affect our relationships and behavior, and we must form strategies to reduce their impact.

Narrative:

A carpenter had just finished a tough day in his workshop. His electric saw had broken down and he had lost an hour of labor, and when he climbed into his truck, it wouldn't start. I offered him a ride home in my car. We drove in silence, but when we arrived, he invited me in to meet his family. Just before he stepped onto his porch, he delicately brushed both of his hands against the branches of a small tree in the yard. Then when he opened his front door, his aspect was immediately transformed. His face broke into a huge smile, he hugged his children, and kissed his wife. At the end of my visit, he walked me back to my car. As we passed the tree, my curiosity got the better of me and I asked him why his attitude changed when we arrived.

"Oh, that's my Tree of Problems," he replied. "I know I can't avoid having problems at work, but I never take them home with me to bother my wife and children. I simply hang them on the branches of this tree every night and pick them up in the morning as I leave the house."

✳ Reflecting on this narrative

- What do you think of the carpenter's strategy?

- Do you think that sometimes we take our problems from school, work, or elsewhere home with us?

- Do you think it is important to protect the emotional weather in your home?

- Have you ever found that if you let a problem "rest," when you return to it later it can seem less important or has changed into an inconvenience? Can you think of any examples?

- Do you consider it fair to unload your accumulated ill humor, stress, and other problems on your family or others around you?

- Do you think that it would be a good idea to declare your home an "emotional preservation area"? How could this work?

✳ Conclusions and other considerations

Every day we accumulate tension and emotional trash. We should understand that we are responsible for managing these residual emotions and should not unload them on the people around us.

Our home must become an emotionally protected zone. Before we step over the threshold, it is essential that we practice a high level of affective hygiene, separating our emotional trash (stress, ill humor, bitterness, or impotence) from our ecological emotions (love, tenderness, gratitude, happiness). In this way we will not entangle one with the other.

We can form a mental image of our own Tree of Problems and metaphorically hang our worries on its branches. This way we will avoid contaminating those around us and ensure that we are emotionally clean as we interact with them.

AND IF WE FILTER IT?

Objective:

Learn to filter information so that we are able to detect and eliminate its toxicity and avoid emotional contagion and contamination, working together to improve the emotional climate.

Narrative:

The story goes that a disciple returned home to his mentor and proclaimed:

"Master, they say that a friend has been saying bad things about you."

"Wait!" interrupted his mentor. "Have you used the three filters before telling me this?"

"Which three filters?" asked the disciple.

"The first is the filter of truth. Are you sure that what you are telling me is the truth?"

"Well, I didn't hear it directly. Some neighbors told me about it."

"Then have you at least used the second filter?" quizzed the maestro. "The filter of kindness? Do you think that what you are saying to me will benefit anyone?"

"No, I suppose not. The opposite, in fact."

"Aha! So then we must apply the final filter: the filter of necessity. Do you think you really need to tell me what is troubling you?"

"Actually, no."

"Then," concluded the maestro with a smile "If something is not the truth, kind, or necessary, it is better that we cast it forever into the void."

Reflecting on this narrative

- Do you know what a rumor is?

- Has anyone ever said bad things about you behind your back? How did you feel? Which emotions did you experience?

- Have you ever said bad things about another person?

- Why do you think we do this?

- What can happen if we spread a false rumor about someone?

- Do you think there might be more than one truth for the same situation?

- Does spreading a rumor benefit anyone?

- Do you think that by not spreading rumors and instead applying the filters of truth, kindness, and necessity, we can help to improve the emotional climate?

Conclusions and other considerations

We must all work together to reduce emotional contamination. It is important to always remember this principle of emotional ecology: what you do not want done to yourself, do not do to others.

If we harm someone with our reckless behavior, then we must repair any damage that we have caused. This will heal the emotional wounds we have inflicted on others as well as ourselves.

THE DECONTAMINATION SQUAD

✻ Objective:

To recognize words that are sources of suffering and emotional contamination, learn how to use them less often, and learn how to recycle or replace them so they do not make the emotional weather worse.

Exercise:

This exercise requires magazines, newspapers, paper, scissors, glue, and paint.

For this group activity, participants will "clean" contaminating words from published articles they have collected. Their search will focus only on headlines and text highlighted in the articles.

Form groups and instruct each group to look for the words that they think damage or contaminate emotional weather. They will cut them out and glue them to a piece of paper, forming a collage.

Each group reads out loud the words that have been selected. They could list them on a separate sheet of paper to better present them to the rest of the class

Next, each group chooses five polluting words or phrases and substitutes them with emotionally clean and responsible equivalents. The entire group should collaborate on this.

Play some background music and ask the groups to remain silent as they take turns putting their contaminated papers through an electric shredder.

Use the strips of shredded paper to create a sculpture that symbolizes emotional hygiene.

✻ Reflecting on this exercise

- What did you learn during this activity?
- Do we always say what we think?
- Have you ever hurt somebody with a word? Which word?
- Have you ever healed somebody with a word? Which word?
- What three words or phrases that you found do you consider the most contaminating?
- Was it difficult for you to "clean" them?
- Do you think it would be a good idea to have a verbal decontamination squad in your classroom?

✻ Conclusions and other considerations

Words are powerful. They can heal, console, and gladden, or injure, discourage, and contaminate. Words can be darts that hurt us or a balm that cures us.

When we talk without thinking about what we are saying, we affect the emotional weather by releasing emotional toxins into the air around us. It is also irresponsible to write without considering the impact our words will have.

If we really want to improve our selves and relationships and live in a peaceful and better world, we must use considered, cleaner, ecological, and responsible language.

EMOTIONAL FIRST-AID KIT

Objective:

To work on the fourth "R" of emotional sustainability: repair. To be aware that all the objects in our emotional first-aid kit can be found inside us.

Exercise:

Form four groups and give each group a worksheet with the following instructions:

Think about what you will include in your emotional first-aid kit. First, make a list of the supplies that we find in a medical first-aid kit: band-aids, scissors, gauze, iodine, burn ointment, a thermometer, etc. Investigate what they are used for and write down your findings.

Then invent the products you would use in your emotional first-aid kit. For example: an ointment that heals emotional wounds or pills that alleviate the suffering of others. Use your imagination, because after listing and illustrating your ideas, you will present the contents of your first-aid kit to your classmates. You must also include written accounts of situations in which each of your products can be used.

Once the kits are ready, each group presents their pictures and explains their contents to the class, including instructions on how to use each component in case of emergency.

Reflecting on this exercise

- What can you use to cheer yourself up when you are feeling sad?
- What would you put in your first-aid kit to cure a dose of "I'm no use for anything"?
- What could you use a boxful of kisses for?
- Would a thermometer that measured anger be useful?
- What do you think are three phrases that make you feel better?
- Do you say and hear them often?
- What could you cut with magic emotional scissors?
- When could you use special glue that fixes broken hearts?
- What music that promotes a sense of well-being would you stow in your kit?
- If you had to include a photograph of something heartwarming and beautiful, what would it be?

Conclusions and other considerations

Living beings are both sensitive and conscious. We are vulnerable; we can damage ourselves and those around us. But the solution is not to isolate or fight among ourselves, nor to create shells in which to hide.

It is important that we learn to protect, care for, and heal ourselves, preparing for any occasion in which we feel damaged.

If we recognize our own qualities and resources, we can successfully relate to and trust in those around us. Our first-aid kit is something invisible that we must always maintain in good condition. It is of no use to us if the boxes and jars inside are empty.

When others hurt us, it is important that we tend to our wounds, clean out emotional toxins, and help them heal with a dose of forgiveness ointment.

ABOUT THE AUTHORS

Maria Mercè Conangla and **Jaume Soler** are psychologists and creators of Fundació Àmbit (Institute for Personal Growth), Barcelona, a nonprofit organization that since 1996 has provided training, counseling, and resources for personal growth and emotional education and management. Two of its most innovative offerings are the *ÀMBIT universit@rtdelviure* and the *master's in emotional ecology degree program*, which the authors co-direct. In 2002, their research and work in humanist psychology inspired them to create the new concept of emotional ecology, which they've developed in more than eleven books. The authors give frequent talks and teach master's level courses at the University of Barcelona.

www.ecologiaemocional.org | www.fundacioambit.org

Other Schiffer Books by the Author:
Emotional Explorers: A Creative Approach to Managing Emotions,
ISBN: 978-0-7643-5553-0
Relationship Navigators: A Creative Approach to Managing Emotions,
ISBN: 978-0-7643-5555-4

Other Schiffer Books on Related Subjects:
Unraveling Rose by Brian Wray,
ISBN: 978-0-7643-5393-2
Meditative Zendoodles: A Treasure Trove of Relaxing Moments by Susanne Schaadt,
ISBN: 978-0-7643-5289-8

Originally published as Cómo está el Clima! by ParramónPaidotribo, Badalona, Spain
©2014 ParramónPaidotribo
Translated from the Spanish by Ian Hayden Jones.

Library of Congress Control Number: 2018937049

Designed by: Jack Chappell
Cover Design by: Molly Shields
Editorial Direction: María Fernanda Canal
Illustrations: Paloma Valdivia
Edition: Cristina Vilella
Type set in: Stereofidelic/Jivetalk/Freehand575/Interstate

ISBN: 978-0-7643-5624-7
Printed in China

Published by Schiffer Publishing, Ltd.
4880 Lower Valley Road
Atglen, PA 19310
Phone: (610) 593-1777; Fax: (610) 593-2002
E-mail: Info@schifferbooks.com
Web: www.schifferbooks.com

For our complete selection of fine books on this and related subjects, please visit our website at www.schifferbooks.com. You may also write for a free catalog.

Schiffer Publishing's titles are available at special discounts for bulk purchases for sales promotions or premiums. Special editions, including personalized covers, corporate imprints, and excerpts, can be created in large quantities for special needs. For more information, contact the publisher.

We are always looking for people to write books on new and related subjects. If you have an idea for a book, please contact us at proposals@schifferbooks.com.